Meow!
Will you answer
the call for adventure?

Kitty

and the
Great Lantern Race

Greenwillow Books
An Imprint of HarperCollins Publishers

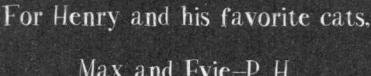

For Henry and his favorite cats,
Max and Evie–P. H.

For Clare and Lizzie, the best team!–J. L.

Kitty and the Great Lantern Race
Text copyright © 2020 by Paula Harrison. Illustrations copyright © 2020 by Jenny Løvlie
First published in the United Kingdom in 2020 by Oxford University Press; first published in the United States by Greenwillow Books, 2021

www.harpercollinschildrens.com. The text of this book is set in Berling LT Std.

Library of Congress Cataloging-in-Publication Data is available.
ISBN 978-0-06-293580-9 (hardcover) — ISBN 978-0-06-293578-6 (paperback)
21 22 23 24 25 PC/LSCC 10 9 8 7 6 5 4 3 2 1
First edition
 Greenwillow Books

Contents

Meet Kitty & Her Cat Crew

Kitty

Kitty has special powers—but is she ready to be a superhero just like her mom?

Luckily, Kitty's cat crew has faith in her and shows Kitty the hero that lies within.

Pumpkin

A stray ginger kitten who is utterly devoted to Kitty.

Figaro

Wise and kind, Figaro knows the neighborhood like the back of his paw.

Pixie

Pixie has a nose for trouble and whiskers for mischief!

Katsumi

Sleek and sophisticated, Katsumi is quick to call Kitty at the first sign of trouble.

Kitty

and the
Great Lantern Race

Chapter 1

Kitty cut out two pointy cat ears and carefully stuck them on her paper lantern. She smiled, lifting the lantern up by its handle. Tomorrow evening all of Hallam City would celebrate the Festival of Light. There would be a huge parade through the city streets with a beautiful fireworks display at the end.

All around the classroom, children were making different sorts of lanterns. Each one would have a candle-shaped

light bulb placed inside. Kitty couldn't wait to see them all shine in the dark like a mass of twinkling stars. She had made her lantern look like a cat's face, using black and white paper and long whiskers

3

made from black pipe cleaners. It looked a little bit like her cat friend Figaro!

Kitty had a special reason for making a cat-shaped lantern. She had amazing catlike superpowers, and she was training to be a real superhero. She often went out in the moonlight to have adventures with her cat crew, leaping and somersaulting across the city's roofs. Kitty loved feeling her special powers tingling inside her. She also loved being with her cat friends, especially Pumpkin, the roly-poly ginger kitten who slept on her bed every night.

Emily, who sat across from Kitty in class, tapped her on the arm. "Look, Kitty! Do you like my butterfly?" She showed Kitty her lantern, which had bright purple wings edged with silver sparkles, and delicate green antennae.

"That looks beautiful!" Kitty said admiringly.

Emily beamed. "I can't wait till tomorrow. The lantern parade is going to be amazing. My mom and dad are coming to watch with my aunt Sarah."

Kitty's heart sank a little as she remembered that her parents wouldn't be there. Her mom, who was a superhero herself, would be working, and her dad didn't want to keep her little brother, Max, up too late. But at least she would be with her school friends, and maybe the cat crew would come to watch, too!

"It's going to be brilliant!" Kitty agreed. "I wonder who will win the prize this year."

"I hope it's someone from our class," said Emily.

Every school in Hallam City took part in the lantern parade, and at the

end, there was a prize for the best lantern. This year, the prize would be a magnificent crown decorated with a gleaming golden star. Their teacher, Mrs. Phillips, had brought the crown in to show them, and it was standing on her desk at the front of the classroom, glittering in the sunlight. They had worked extra hard on their lanterns once they'd seen how beautiful it was.

Mrs. Phillips clapped her hands. "The lanterns

8

look wonderful, everyone! You may take them home with you today, but don't forget to bring them to the festival tomorrow night."

Kitty picked up her lantern by its handle and smiled. She couldn't wait to show her lamp to her family and all her cat friends.

When darkness fell, Kitty switched on the candlelight bulb inside her lantern and placed it on her bedroom windowsill. She hoped lots of the cat crew would visit tonight. Then she

could tell them all about the
Festival of Light, and ask them
if they'd like to watch her in
the lantern parade.

She watched the moon rise, casting a silvery glow over the roofs of the houses. The sky darkened and the swaying tree branches sent shadows dancing across the walls. Hundreds of stars began to appear, glittering like tiny diamonds.

Pumpkin, who was curled up on Kitty's bed, gave a huge yawn. "Aren't you tired yet, Kitty?"

"Not yet!" Kitty smiled. "Do you think Figaro and the others will come to see us tonight?"

Pumpkin stretched and leaped

onto the window seat to join Kitty. He nuzzled her arm before staring out at the dark. "I can't see any sign of them. No, wait! Is there something by the top of that chimney?"

Kitty opened the window a little, and the night breeze ruffled the curtains. Her catlike superpowers rushed through her body, making her skin tingle. Using her special nighttime vision and super hearing, she peered into the dark. Suddenly everything looked sharp and clear, and she could hear dozens of tiny sounds, from a car whooshing past to a tiny moth fluttering beside a streetlamp.

She turned her attention to the

distant rooftops. A black cat with a white face and paws ran jauntily along the peak of a roof. Scampering in front of him was a fluffy white cat with bright green eyes.

"Figaro and Pixie are coming!" Kitty told Pumpkin, and the ginger kitten's stripy tail swished excitedly.

"Good evening, Kitty!" called Figaro,

when he reached her windowsill. "Well, that is a fine-looking lantern. Did you make it yourself?"

"Yes, I did! It's for the Festival of Light tomorrow." Kitty explained all about the lantern parade and the fireworks. "So I hoped you might come and watch me from a nearby rooftop."

"I didn't know there would be fireworks." Pumpkin trembled and put one paw to his cheek. "Maybe I should stay here instead . . ."

"I don't like them, either. They make such horrible bangs and crashes!" Pixie agreed. "Don't worry, Pumpkin. I'll stay here and look after you."

"Fireworks are such a nuisance!" said Figaro, twirling his whiskers. "Perhaps I will also stay behind. But I hope you have a wonderful time in the parade, Kitty. Maybe your lantern will win that amazing prize!"

Kitty swallowed her disappointment.

She should have remembered that lots of cats hated fireworks. But at least this way Pumpkin would have friends around to look after him. "I'll tell you all about it when I get back," she promised. "I think it'll be a night to remember!"

Chapter 2

The following evening, Kitty fizzed with excitement as she joined the crowds of children taking part in the parade. The full moon shined brightly, and the streets were full of people. Long gold and red streamers hung

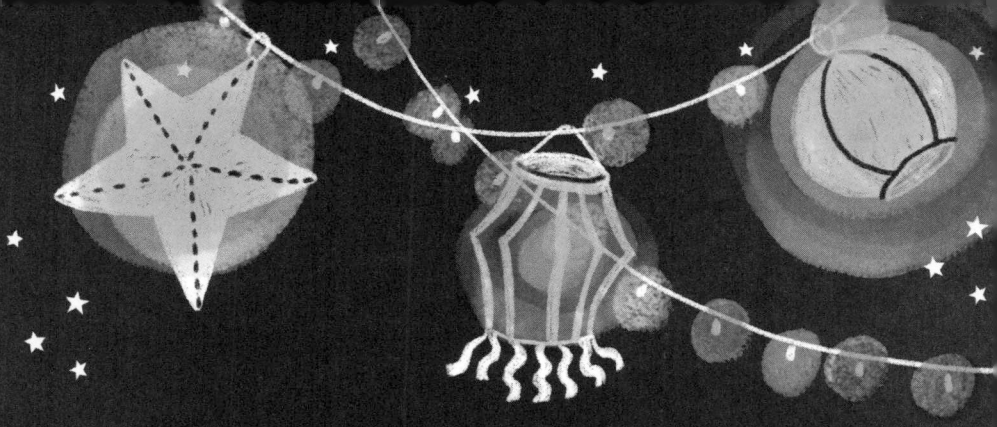

between the lampposts, and glowing lamps dangled from the trees like magical golden fruit. A frosty breeze blew gently along the road, and Kitty zipped her coat up tight.

Emily linked arms with Kitty. "There are so many people here! And look at all these lanterns."

Kitty spotted a train lantern and a

23

unicorn one with a shiny horn. There are so many different ones!" She smiled at her friend. "But I still think your butterfly lantern is the best."

Mrs. Phillips called everyone over,

and the parade began. Everyone lit their lanterns and together the crowd moved forward, the lights bobbing like an enormous, sparkly caterpillar. Spectators lined the streets, clapping as

25

the group of children went past.

Kitty beamed. It was wonderful to be part of something so spectacular. She looked around at all the people and the lights. She wanted to be able to describe everything to Pumpkin, Pixie, and Figaro when she got home.

A movement on a nearby rooftop caught her eye. She glanced up and saw a black shape darting past a chimney. Moonlight

reflected from a nearby satellite dish. When Kitty looked at the rooftop again, the figure was gone.

The parade moved on, reaching a bend in the road, and the streamers on the lampposts fluttered in the breeze.

"My watch is missing!" shouted a man in the crowd.

Kitty looked over at once. A gray-haired man was staring at his arm in shock. He checked his pockets before searching the ground around his feet.

28

"Where is it?" he cried. "I felt something brush against my arm, and then my watch was gone!"

"Maybe the strap broke and it fell off," said the man next to him.

The gray-haired man shook his head vigorously. "No, I'm sure it didn't! I bought it just last week, and the strap is very strong. I don't understand it!"

Kitty frowned. It seemed very odd that someone's watch would disappear like that. As the parade moved on, she watched the crowd carefully. Her night vision picked up every tiny movement in the darkness, and she used her super hearing to focus on any strange sounds.

She glimpsed a shadowy figure slipping past a shop's doorway. Kitty tried to keep track of the shadow, but it seemed to melt away into the mass of people. A moment later, a woman in a furry white coat gave a terrible shriek. "My ruby necklace . . . it's gone!"

Kitty dashed through the crowd. "What happened?" she asked the

lady. "Could the necklace have fallen off?"

"I don't think so." The woman clutched her neck. "I felt

something . . . like a brush of fur against my throat. Then I looked down and my precious string of red rubies was gone!"

Kitty looked around quickly. Everyone standing close to the lady looked just as confused as she did.

"My husband gave me that necklace when we got married, so it's very important to me." Tears formed in the woman's eyes. "Who could have done such a horrible thing?"

Kitty held her lantern tightly. There was something suspicious about all this.

The watch and the ruby necklace had both disappeared very suddenly, and that made her think it wasn't an accident. But who had taken them . . . and how?

Kitty knew she wanted to help. She was a superhero in training, after all! Her stomach felt strange, as if there were moths fluttering inside it. Was this really a good idea? She didn't have any of her cat crew to help her this time. Pumpkin and the others were far away at home. She would be investigating the missing watch and necklace all by herself. How would she manage it all alone?

She took a deep breath. Her superhero skills were needed right now, so she had to find a way! She remembered what her

34

mom had told her the first time she went on a moonlight adventure: *Don't let fear hold you back. You're braver than you think!* She just had to do her best.

Kitty hurried back to Emily's side. "A lady's necklace has vanished, and I have to go and help," she told her friend. "Would you look after my lantern?"

"Of course I will!" Emily took the cat lantern. "Will you be all right?"

Kitty smiled bravely. "Don't worry about me! I'm going to look around and see what I can find out."

"Good luck!" said Emily, her eyes wide.

Kitty slipped away from the crowd and into the shadows. Hiding behind a tree, she threw off her coat to reveal her cat superhero outfit underneath. Her cape unfurled in the night breeze. She was glad she'd put it on before going out tonight. It was always good to be prepared!

Pulling her superhero mask out of her pocket, she put it on and looked around in the gloom. Was the shadowy figure she'd spotted connected to the disappearing watch and necklace? She didn't know for sure, but if she was right, someone could be stealing people's belongings while they were busy watching the lantern parade.

If that was true, then it had to be someone very sneaky who could slip in and out of the crowd without anyone noticing. She had to stop them before they stole even more valuables.

Kitty felt a rush of energy. She darted over to a streetlight and shinnied up the post to get a better view. From there, she could see over the top of the crowd. The parade was moving on, and dozens of lanterns bobbed up and down in the darkness. The spectators clapped and the red and gold streamers flapped in the wind. Kitty frowned. Where was that strange figure?

Suddenly, she spotted a pair of amber eyes watching her from behind a mailbox on the other side of the street. A black mask covered the figure's face, but her sharp eyes were full of mischief. Before Kitty could get a better look, the shadowy figure moved on, slipping through the crowd and dodging around lampposts.

Kitty's skin tingled. She had a funny feeling deep down that she had just found the jewel thief!

Chapter 3

Kitty leaped down from the lamppost, landing gracefully on the pavement. The escaping thief darted through the crowd, jumping over trash cans. Kitty chased her down the street, her superpowers tingling through her body.

The robber was still a long way ahead, but Kitty was sure she could catch her.

The thief glanced around, her eyes glinting. She laughed when she saw Kitty chasing her. Then she swooped into the crowd and snatched a handbag from a lady's arm, before hiding behind the next lamppost. The lady clutched her shoulder and looked around in alarm.

"Hey!" cried Kitty. "Give that back."

The thief ignored Kitty's command. Slippery as a shadow, she vanished

into the
crowd and
appeared
again on
the opposite
side of the
road.

Kitty ran even faster.
Leaping onto a bench, she
grabbed hold of a tree branch
and used it to swing herself across

the street. She landed neatly and kept on running. The thief was just ahead, dodging a trash can. Then she ducked

behind a line of people and disappeared again.

Kitty looked around desperately and noticed something moving overhead. The robber had climbed a long drainpipe leading up the side of a building. Springing onto the rooftop, she turned and shook the handbag triumphantly at Kitty. A string of

rubies glittered around her neck. Then she scampered across the roof, headed in the same direction as the lantern parade.

Kitty pulled herself skillfully up the drainpipe, one hand after the other. There was something really strange about this thief. She was very small and fast, and she seemed used to heights. She didn't seem to

care about how many people she robbed.
Kitty was determined to catch the crook
before she ruined the whole festival.

An icy wind spun across the rooftop,
making Kitty's cape swirl. She ran lightly
along the ridge of the roof, following
the thief as she jumped the narrow gap

between two buildings. Below them the
parade went on its way, and the streets
were full of noise and laughter.

Kitty felt very alone on the rooftop.
She thought of all the times her friends
had helped her and cheered her on. She

wished she had Figaro or Pixie or any of her cat crew to keep her company.

She took a deep breath. There must be a way to outsmart this villain. She might be planning to swoop down to the street and rob someone else in the crowd. Maybe Kitty could take a shortcut and catch the robber as she returned to the rooftop.

Kitty hid behind a chimney. Then, when she was sure the thief wasn't looking, she climbed from a window ledge to the ground. Racing along the street, a little farther on she climbed back to the rooftop. If this plan worked, she could catch the robber by surprise! She peered down at the crowd, expecting to see the shadowy figure.

The crowd went on clapping. People's voices drifted up from the street below. Kitty caught sight of Emily carrying the butterfly and cat lanterns. Kitty balanced at the edge of the roof, watching and waiting.

The parade was moving toward a brightly lit platform at the end of the

street. The mayor of
Hallam City stood waiting
there, dressed in her best clothes.
Kitty used her special vision to look
more closely. The mayor was holding
the golden crown—the prize for

the best lantern—and its beautiful star decoration gleamed in the light. It would be given out during a special ceremony at the end of the parade.

A shadow moved on a rooftop right beside the platform. Kitty felt a flutter

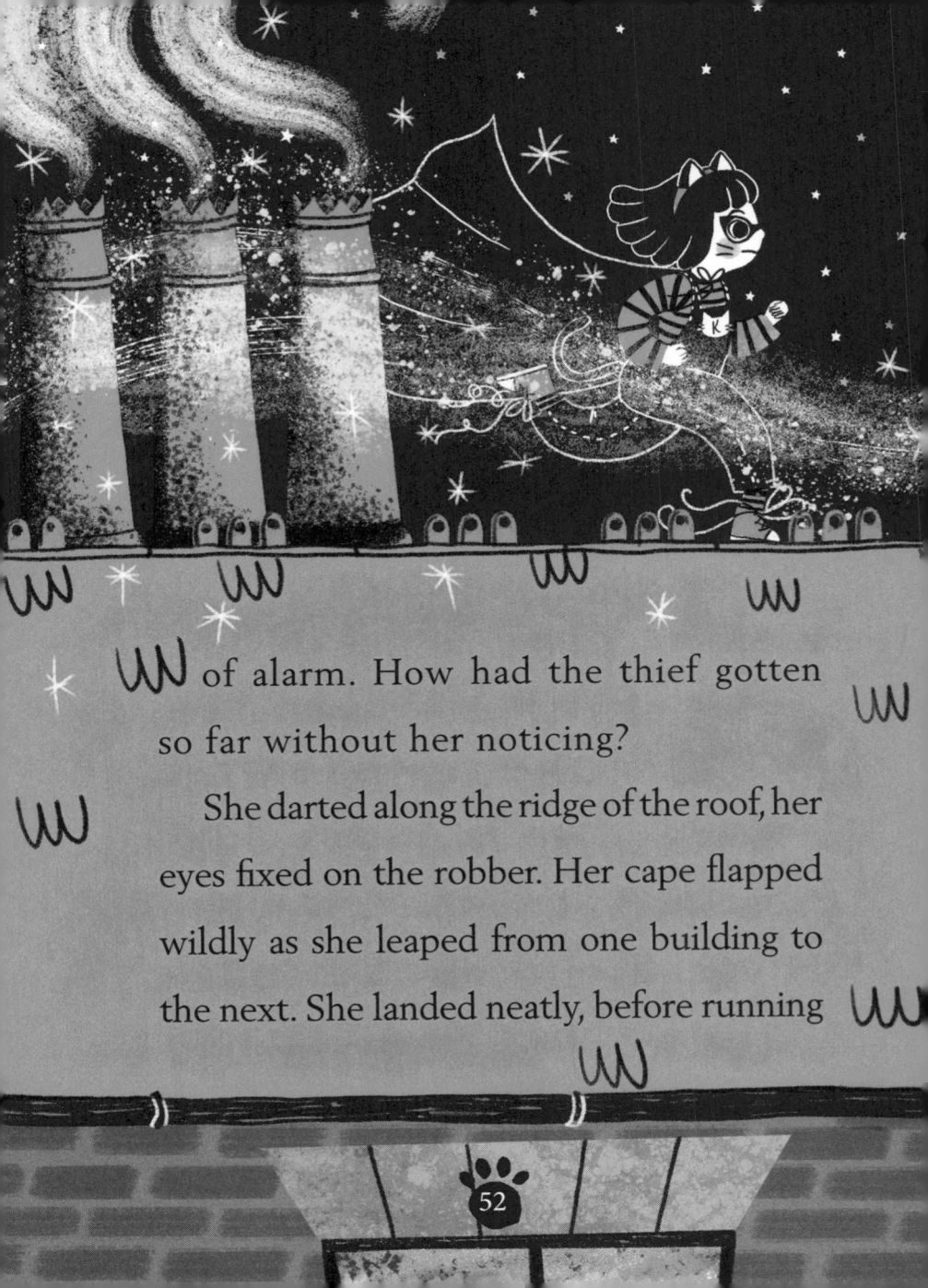

of alarm. How had the thief gotten so far without her noticing?

She darted along the ridge of the roof, her eyes fixed on the robber. Her cape flapped wildly as she leaped from one building to the next. She landed neatly, before running

on past a row of chimneys.

The thief swung down a nearby drainpipe and made a graceful leap to the ground. Then she crept closer to the stage, prowling in and out of the shadows. Everyone in the crowd was smiling at the children in the lantern parade. None of them had seen the shadowy figure moving toward the platform.

The thief's gaze was fixed on the mayor. Kitty's heart sank. She must be after the golden crown!

With a burst of energy, Kitty ran faster than ever. The wind whistled past her ears and her cape streamed out behind her. She jumped from rooftop to rooftop. Then she swung down a drainpipe before dropping to the ground.

The thief crept up the platform steps.

Her sharp amber eyes spotted Kitty at the edge of the crowd, and she laughed.

"Stop!" cried Kitty. "You can't take the prize. You'll ruin the whole festival!" But her voice was lost among the clapping and cheering of the crowd.

The robber tiptoed up behind the mayor, and for a second, Kitty got a clear

view of the shadowy figure. There was something very familiar about her graceful movements and her pricked-up ears. Then the thief snatched the crown from the mayor before leaping off the platform and disappearing down an alleyway.

The mayor stared down in surprise at her empty hands. A murmur of shock swept across the crowd.

"What happened to the crown?" asked a woman close to Kitty.

"I think someone took

it!" gasped the man next to her.

The parade came to a stop, and the children with the lanterns bumped into one another. Some of them pointed to the mayor as they passed along the bad news about the missing crown. A small boy with a dinosaur lantern burst into tears.

"It's not just the crown that's vanished," one lady called out. "That thief took my handbag, too!"

"And my watch!' shouted a man. "Maybe there's a whole gang of robbers here tonight."

The buzz of the crowd grew louder, and Kitty's teacher, Mrs. Phillips, climbed the steps to the platform and talked hurriedly to the mayor. At last, the mayor stepped forward and held up her hand for quiet. "Please, everyone, stay calm! I don't know what's happening to our lovely festival, but I will do my best to find out."

Kitty's heart thumped. None of them had really seen the robber except for her. She

had to find that thief and get the crown back! She peered down the alley where the crook had vanished. Then she straightened her superhero mask before running into the dark.

Chapter 4

Kitty raced down the alley. The noise of the crowd faded as she ran farther away from the festival. She stopped at a corner and listened carefully for any tiny sounds. The wind whistled gently down the moonlit street, and there was the distant hoot of an owl. A cluster of fallen leaves danced in the night breeze.

Quick footsteps came from another alley not far away. Kitty followed the faint sound, hoping it was the thief. She zigzagged through the maze of streets and alleys. Every now and then, the footsteps stopped, and Kitty paused too. It would be easier to catch the thief if she didn't know Kitty was following her.

The next alley opened on to a wide road full of shops and restaurants. Moonlight glinted like frost on the shop

windows. A sign in a café window read

DELICIOUS SOUPS AND SANDWICHES SERVED

ALL DAY. The Hallam Wonder Tower, the

tallest building in the whole city, rose

into the night like a vast stone giant.

Kitty waited and waited, but there

were no more footsteps. Had the thief

realized she was following? Was she

hiding around a corner in the dark?

62

Something twinkled on the Wonder Tower. There was a tiny dark shape about five floors up, moving very slowly, like an ant crawling up a branch. Kitty stared in shock. The thief looked small because she was so high, and the glinting light was the star on the golden crown, shining in the moonlight.

Kitty's heart fluttered. She knew her

superpowers would help her . . . but did she really want to go all the way up there? The Wonder Tower was enormous. It had a place to eat at the top called the Cloud Restaurant, and above that, a metal radio mast jutted into the sky. Kitty could see the top of the mast, with its flashing red light that warned away airplanes.

She shivered. Maybe the tower was too high, even for someone with special powers. But there were stolen handbags and necklaces that had to be taken back to their owners . . . and how could the lantern competition go ahead with no prize? She thought of the disappointed faces of her classmates. Hurrying to the bottom of the tower, she began to climb.

She had to work hard to find handholds and footholds on the smooth stone building, and the higher she went, the stronger the wind became. Kitty looked up just as the thief disappeared through an open window on the sixth floor. She must be planning to hide somewhere inside, Kitty thought.

Kitty climbed to the sixth floor and dropped through the same window. She was standing on a staircase with long flights of steps leading up and down. Quick footsteps sounded overhead. Kitty followed the steps upward, treading as quietly as she could.

The stairs wound on and on. Kitty

counted the floors . . . nine, ten, eleven . . .
twenty-four, twenty-five, twenty-six.
She lost count at around the

fortieth floor, but a minute later she found herself on the final set of steps. A magnificent set of doors, with the name

Cloud Restaurant

in big gold letters, stood at the top.

Kitty hesitated. The thief must have gone inside. She crept a little closer.

There was a sudden whirring sound from inside the restaurant. Kitty warily opened the door and spotted an elegant striped cat sitting on a stool at the counter. Her long tail flicked as she drank from a tall glass through a stripy red straw. The festival crown, the handbag, and all the other loot was on the countertop.

Kitty held back a gasp. So the thief was a cat! That was why she'd climbed buildings so easily and leaped so gracefully from one roof to the next. Kitty had to admit that the cat burglar was the most nimble creature she'd ever seen, and one of the sneakiest, too. But how dare she sit there relaxing after spoiling the parade!

Creeping up silently, Kitty dived at the thief and grabbed her before she could escape.

The robber jumped in surprise, and her drink sprayed all over the counter. "Hey, what's going on? Who are you?"

"I'm Kitty, and I've come to take back all the things you've stolen!" said Kitty. "You should be ashamed of yourself." She spun the thief around to face her and pulled off the cat's mask. Underneath were a set of elegant whiskers, a cute black nose, and mischievous amber eyes.

"You caught me! No one's ever done that before. My name's Dodger, by the way!" The cat grinned and held out a furry paw. Her tail swayed gracefully.

Kitty let go of her,

frowning. This cat didn't seem bothered by being caught at all. Why didn't she look upset or even guilty?

Dodger lifted her glass again and slurped through the stripy straw. "I can make you some of this drink if you'd like, Kitty. Mango-and-fish smoothies are my favorite!"

Kitty shook her head. This wasn't going the way she'd expected. "Why are you here? Are you stealing from the restaurant?"

"I live here! The cook lets me sleep

under the tables, and sometimes the customers give me their chicken or fish to eat. I love being high up. It makes me feel like I can do anything!" Dodger scampered over to the window and waved her paw at the bright full moon smiling down on the city below. "See

that view? It's the best in the city!"

Kitty followed her to the window. The whole of Hallam City was spread out below them in a carpet of little twinkling lights. Kitty could just about make out the park near her house and the clock tower where she'd first met Pumpkin.

The whole city
had a magical, silvery look
in the moonlight.

"Hey, you should come and live
here with me!" Dodger continued.
"It's so much fun, and you have all
the right cat skills to be part
of my crew."

"You're right—it's amazing here," Kitty agreed. "But I already have a cat crew, and we do things to help people, not hurt them."

Dodger snorted. "That sounds really boring!"

"It's not boring—it's important work. I would never steal anything. Don't you realize you've upset so many people tonight?"

Dodger flicked her tail. "What do you mean? I was only having fun."

"It's not fun to steal other people's

things," said Kitty sternly. "The lady with the ruby necklace said her husband gave her those jewels on the day they got married. They were very special to her."

Dodger looked a little downcast. Then her amber eyes gleamed. "But what about this?" She bounded back to the counter and put the festival crown on her head. "This

didn't really belong to anyone, and see how great it looks on me!" The crown slipped sideways over her velvety-black ear.

For a moment Kitty wanted to laugh, but she stopped herself. "Taking that crown was the *worst* thing you did! It was supposed to be the prize at the end of the festival. Lots of children will be disappointed that it's gone."

"That's stupid! I think you're just trying to ruin all my fun," cried Dodger, shooting Kitty a cross look. Then she snatched up all her loot and raced out of the restaurant.

Kitty dashed after her, but by the time she reached the stairs, the slippery cat thief was gone.

Chapter 5

Kitty rushed down the steps looking for Dodger. Halfway down she stopped and listened, but everything was silent. How had Dodger disappeared so fast?

It took a long time for Kitty to reach the bottom floor, and just as she got there, the elevator door slid closed. Dodger must have come down in the elevator before escaping into the night.

Kitty opened a window and climbed out onto the pavement. A cloud hid the moon, and the street grew darker. Kitty looked along the empty road, frowning. A feeling deep down inside made her follow the alleyway leading back to the festival.

All the chatter and laughter had disappeared from the crowded streets. The children in the lantern parade were waiting close to the mayor's platform. They held their lanterns by their sides, their shoulders slumped. A group of teachers had gathered on the stage to talk to the mayor.

A shadow jumped out at Kitty as she reached the end of the alleyway.

"I know you're following me! Have you come to spoil my fun again?" Dodger scowled. The golden crown still sat lopsided on her head.

"Dodger, you've got to listen to me," said Kitty. "Stealing things isn't fun—

it just makes everyone sad. See that lady over there? She's the one whose handbag you took."

Dodger looked at the lady, who was wiping a tear from her eye.

"And look at my friends!" Kitty went

on. "They spent a long time making their lanterns, and they were having a wonderful time until the prize was taken away."

Kitty's classmates were looking around worriedly, as if they were afraid the thief might return at any moment.

"Does it really look like they're having fun now?" Kitty demanded.

Dodger stared at them and a guilty look spread across

her face. "I guess not! I'm sorry, Kitty. When I left the tower tonight, I just wanted an adventure, so I gave myself a challenge to steal the festival prize. I *love* to test my awesome cat-burglar skills!" She preened her smooth striped fur. "Then when I got here and saw the crowd, it seemed like it would be fun to take the other things too while no one was looking. I didn't think I was hurting anyone."

"Maybe we can fix everything together," suggested Kitty.

Dodger stroked her long whiskers. "Good idea! But how do we do that?"

"All we have to do is give back what you took . . . and if we use our cat skills, it will be just as fun," explained Kitty. "Let's see which of us can return the valuables to their owners the quickest."

Dodger's eyes gleamed. "I accept your challenge! I know I'm bound to be the winner."

Kitty took the lady's handbag and the man's watch and ran down the street. Dodger scampered after her with the ruby necklace and the golden crown.

"Last one to finish is a slowpoke cat!" Dodger called. "Oh . . . and you have to put each thing back without anyone seeing."

"You're on!" Kitty called back. Then she slipped through the crowd and hung the stolen handbag back on the lady's shoulder.

Dodger climbed nimbly up a lamppost and spotted the woman with the ruby necklace on the other side of the crowd. The cat skipped along a

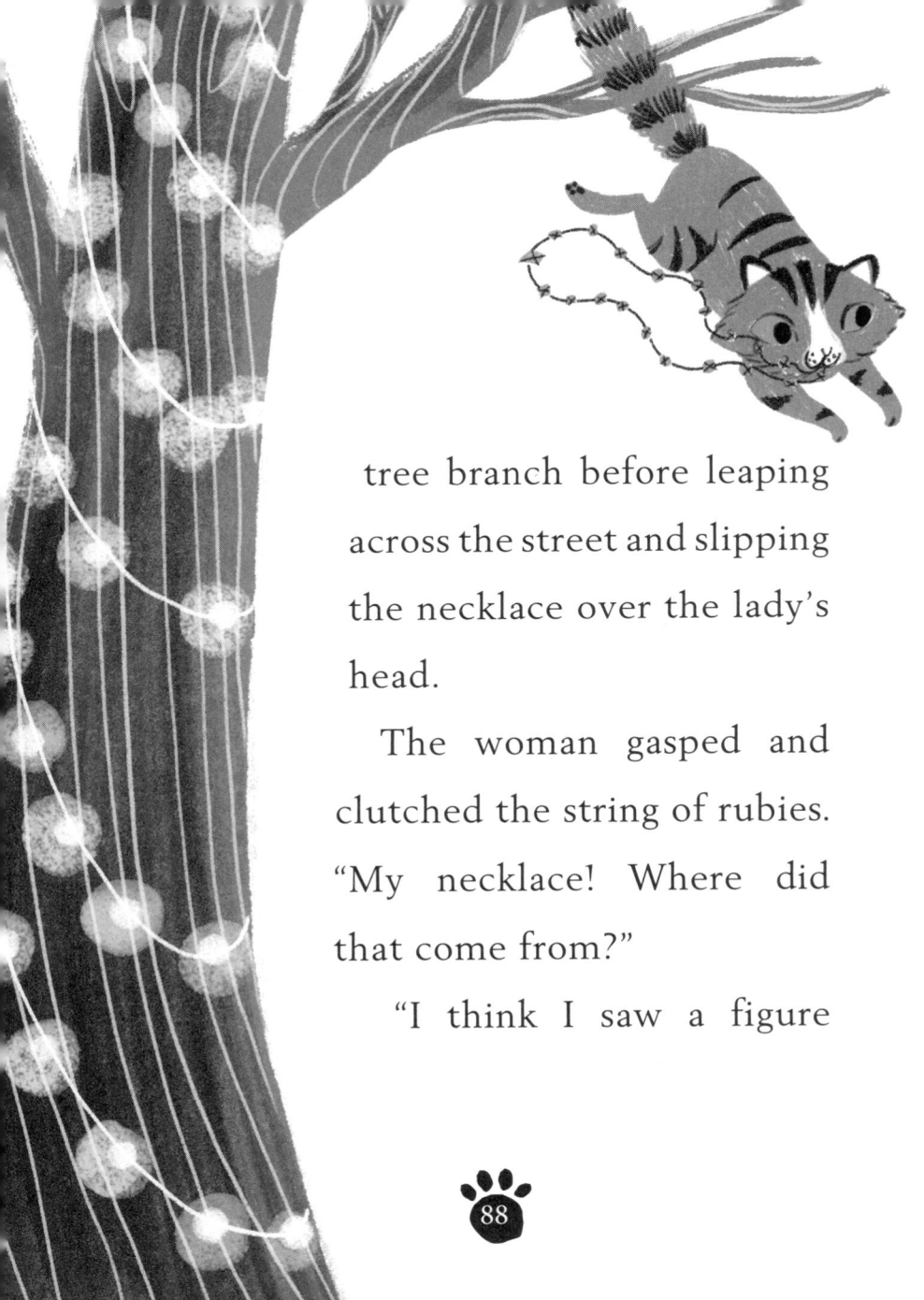

tree branch before leaping across the street and slipping the necklace over the lady's head.

The woman gasped and clutched the string of rubies. "My necklace! Where did that come from?"

"I think I saw a figure

moving over there!" said a man beside her, pointing in the wrong direction.

"It's incredible!" the woman went on. "It just appeared like magic."

Dodger grinned and crept into the darkness of a nearby alley.

Kitty slipped the missing watch onto the wrist of the man it belonged to. She noticed Dodger sneaking onto the platform at the front of the crowd. The wily cat left the crown on a table and disappeared again like a shadow vanishing in the moonlight.

A moment later, Dodger reappeared at Kitty's side, grinning. "That was a lot of fun! But do you think they'll ever

notice that I've put the crown back?"

Kitty smiled. The mayor and the teachers were still busy talking to one another. None of them had noticed the prize laying on the table in the middle of the platform. Then a shout went up as one of the children spotted the crown. A murmur of excitement buzzed around the crowd.

"The prize has been found!" said a dark-haired lady. "Isn't that amazing?"

"That's really good news," replied the man next to her. "I hated seeing the children disappointed."

"So I guess I'm a very good cat after all! *And* I won our competition. I knew I would be the fastest!" Dodger did a

92

triumphant little dance and waved her tail in Kitty's face.

"Well, actually . . ." Kitty was just about to explain that *she'd* finished

93

first, but then she stopped herself. She had a hunch that Dodger wouldn't be a good loser, and this way the cat thief was happy about giving back the stolen things. "I'm very proud of you! Are you going to stay and see them give out the prize for the best lantern?"

"I don't think so." Dodger's tail flicked restlessly. "It's still early, and there might be another adventure waiting for me somewhere!"

Kitty's forehead wrinkled. "You won't steal anything else, will you?

Don't forget how much nicer it is to make people happy."

"Sure—I'll remember!" Dodger winked and smoothed her whiskers. "I hope I'll see you again sometime, Kitty. Come to the Cloud Restaurant if you ever want to try a mango-and-fish smoothie!"

"Thanks, I will! Good luck, Dodger."

Kitty watched the graceful striped cat dart away into the crowd.

Dodger waved to her with a grin, her amber eyes gleaming as she slipped away down an alley.

Kitty waved back, smiling. She'd completed a whole adventure without the help of her cat crew. She couldn't wait to tell her mom all about it! Excitement fluttered in her tummy as the mayor walked to the front of the platform with the golden crown. It looked like the prize was about to be announced!

Chapter 6

Kitty dashed over to join her class. "Thanks for looking after my lantern!" she said to Emily.

"That's okay!" replied Emily. "Did you see what happened? The crown was found again after all."

Kitty nodded, smiling to herself.

Just then, the mayor began to speak. "Ladies and gentlemen! I'm very pleased to say that our prize has been returned, and a big thank-you to anyone who helped get it back. Now I'm going to announce the winner of the lantern competition."

A murmur rippled across the crowd, and everyone watched the mayor eagerly.

"The judges have walked around the parade and looked at all the lanterns carefully," the mayor continued. "There were so many brilliant ones this year and that made it very tricky, but we've decided that the winner is . . . Emily Sanchez, with her butterfly lantern!" The crowd burst into applause. Kitty's whole class cheered, and Emily turned red.

"Go on!" Kitty urged her friend. "You have to go up on the stage and collect your prize."

Emily made her way up the platform steps and shook the mayor's hand. Then she held up her purple butterfly lantern with its silver-edged wings so that everyone could see it properly.

The crowd clapped loudly and the mayor placed the golden crown on Emily's head, saying, "Here's your prize! Very well done, for making such an imaginative and beautiful lantern."

Kitty smiled and cheered. She had been sure that Emily's lantern was

the best one all along! She felt a tap on her shoulder. Spinning around, she found her mom right behind her. "Mom, you made it!" she beamed. "Look! Emily won the lantern competition."

"That's amazing!" Mom put an arm around her shoulder. "I'm sorry I missed the parade. Did you have a wonderful time?"

"Yes, it's been really exciting!" Kitty told her. "The festival prize was stolen, and I had to chase the thief to find it."

"Goodness! I'd love to hear all about it," said Mom.

Together they left the crowd and climbed onto a nearby rooftop. The festival streamers fluttered on the lampposts below, and the lanterns shined brightly.

"Let's find somewhere comfortable to sit," said Kitty's mom. "I think the fireworks are about to start."

They found a comfortable spot beside a chimney just as the fireworks began. Fountains of gold and silver light whooshed into the air before falling down again like glittering rain. Next there were dazzling red and green rockets that shot upward with a loud bang. The night sky filled with sparkling colors as the fireworks soared one after another.

As the last firework burst, Kitty caught a glimpse of Dodger on a distant rooftop. The cat's eyes glinted, and she waved one last time before bounding away into the night.

Kitty told her mom all about Dodger, and how hard she'd worked to catch the naughty cat. "So I went all the way to the top of the Wonder Tower to talk to Dodger. She's quite a cheeky

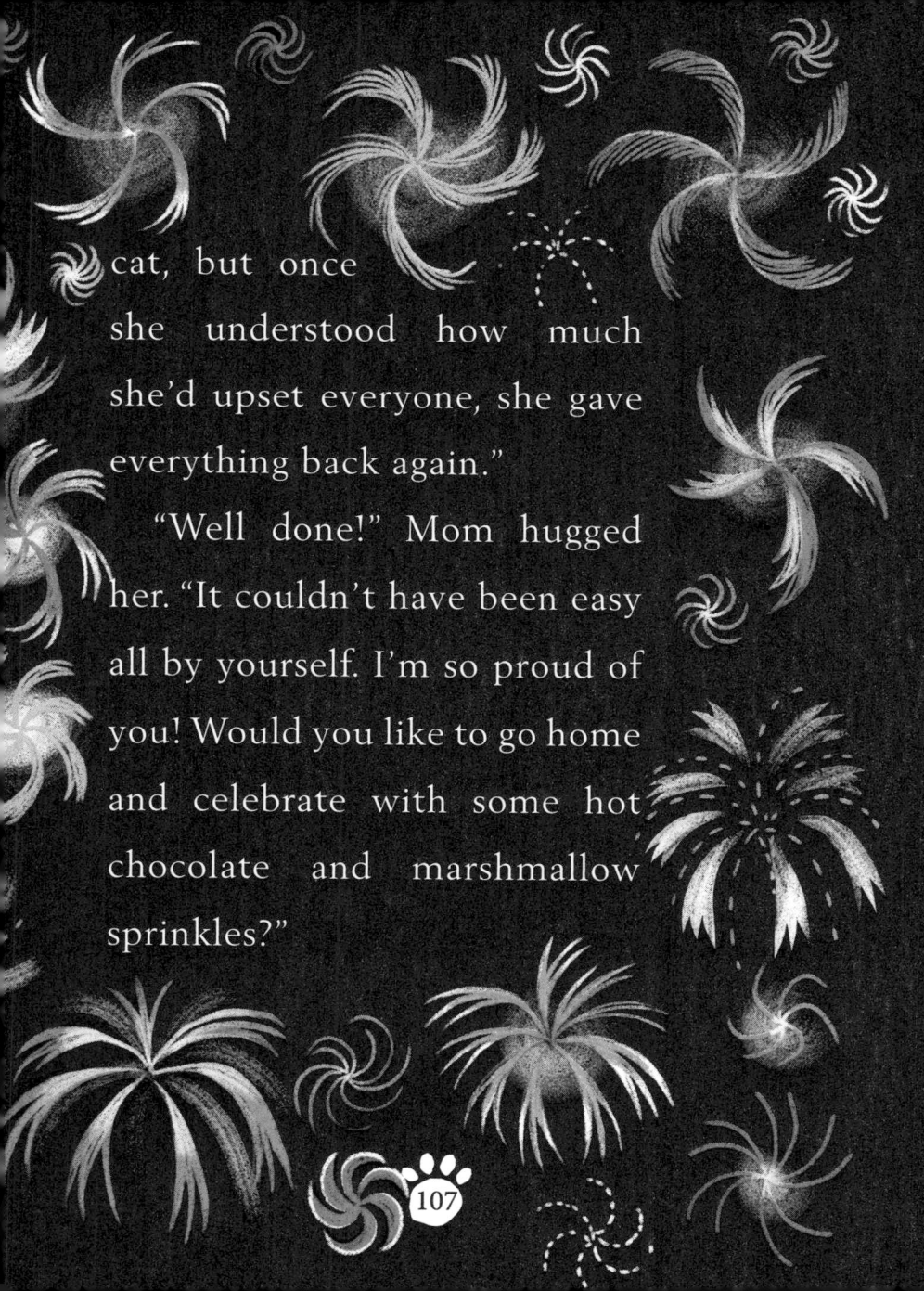

cat, but once she understood how much she'd upset everyone, she gave everything back again."

"Well done!" Mom hugged her. "It couldn't have been easy all by yourself. I'm so proud of you! Would you like to go home and celebrate with some hot chocolate and marshmallow sprinkles?"

"Yes, please!" Kitty watched the last firework soar through the sky like a cluster of shooting stars. Then she went home with her mom, skipping across the rooftops in the moonlight.

Back home there would be hot

chocolate and Pumpkin and her cozy bed. Having an adventure was amazing, but going home afterward was even nicer!

Super Facts About Cats

Super Speed

Have you ever seen a cat make a quick escape from a dog? If so, you know they can move *really* fast—up to thirty miles per hour!

Super Hearing

Cats have an incredible sense of hearing and can swivel their ears to pinpoint even the tiniest of sounds.

Super Reflexes

Have you ever heard the saying, "Cats always land on their feet"? People say this because cats have amazing reflexes. If a cat

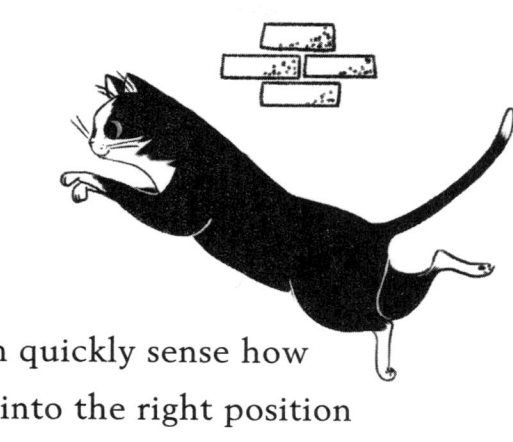

is falling, it can quickly sense how to move its body into the right position to land safely.

Super Vision

Cats have amazing nighttime vision. Their incredible ability to see in low light allows them to hunt for prey when it's dark outside.

Super Smell

Cats have a very powerful sense of smell. Did you know that the pattern of ridges on each cat's nose is as unique as a human's fingerprints?

The Kitty books—
read them all!

Kitty's family has a secret. Her mom is a hero with catlike superpowers, and Kitty knows that one day she'll have special powers and the chance to use them, too. That day comes sooner than expected, when a friendly black cat named Figaro comes to Kitty's bedroom window to ask for help. But the world at night is a scary place— is Kitty brave enough to step out into the darkness for a thrilling moonlight adventure?

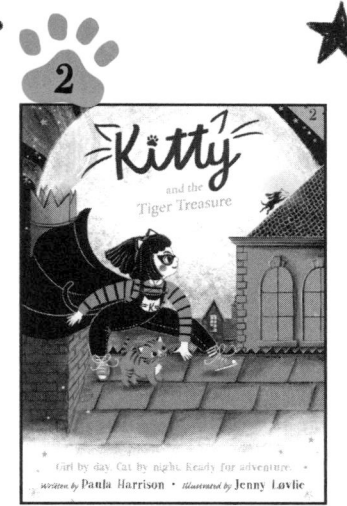

Kitty can't wait to see the priceless Golden Tiger Statue with her own eyes. Legend says that if you hold the statue, you can make your greatest wish come true. Kitty and her cat, Pumpkin, decide to sneak into the museum to see the statue at night, when no one else is around. But disaster strikes when the statue is stolen right in front of them! Can Kitty find the thief and return the precious statue before sunrise?

Kitty, Pumpkin, and Pixie discover a sky garden hidden high on a rooftop. It's a magical place, filled with beautiful flowers and sparkling fairy lights. Pixie is so excited, she wants to tell everyone about it—but the more cats discover the sky garden, the wilder it becomes! Soon the rooftop is overrun with unwelcome visitors. Can Kitty and her friends protect this secret, special place—and all the magical things growing in it—before it's too late?

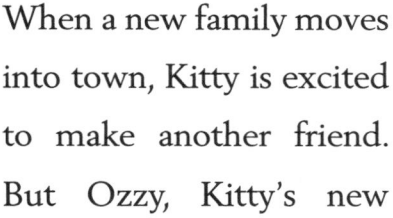

When a new family moves into town, Kitty is excited to make another friend. But Ozzy, Kitty's new neighbor, is quiet and seems to have nothing in common with Kitty. When night approaches, Katsumi, a member of Kitty's cat crew, tells Kitty about a dog causing a commotion in the bakery. Kitty decides to use her catlike superpowers to investigate, and it turns out that Ozzy has his own superpowers, too! Together, they set off to track down the mischievous dog before he can cause even more damage.

Meowing Soon!

Kitty
and the
Twilight Trouble

6

Girl by day. Cat by night. Ready for adventure.

Written by **Paula Harrison** · Illustrated by **Jenny Løvlie**